First published in the United States 1990 by Chronicle Books.
Printed in Hong Kong.   Japan.   Singapore.

Editor's Note: Younger children should only undertake these projects under adult supervision. Parents and teachers should match crafts to the appropriate skill level of the child.

Library of Congress Cataloging-in-Publication Data

Lohf, Sabine.
  [Ich mach was mit Blättern. English]
  Things I can make with leaves : you can make all these
things with leaves / Sabine Lohf.
      p.   cm.
  Translation of: Ich mach was mit Blättern.
  Summary: Presents projects involving making things with
leaves, including leaf people, leaf cards, leaf puppets, and
leaf jewelry.
  ISBN 0-87701-763-8
  1. Nature craft—Juvenile literature.   2. Leaves—Juvenile lit-
erature. [1. Nature craft. 2. Leaves. 3. Handicraft.]
  I. Title
TT873.L6413   1990
745.58'4—dc20   90-31934
                                                    CIP
                                                     AC

10 9 8 7 6 5 4 3 2 1

Chronicle Books
275 Fifth Street
San Francisco, California 94103

Things I Can Make with
LEAVES

Sabine Lohf

You can make all these things with leaves.

Chronicle Books • San Francisco

Leaf Animals

Leaf People

Leaf Cards

Now, that's a nice card.

Glue leaves and flowers to colored paper to make beautiful gift tags or stationery.

Water Lilies

Gently push a flower stem
through the center of a leaf.

You can float them in a bowl of
water or in a pretend pond.

I crown you
King of the frogs!

Grass Dolls

A Flower Crown

This is how to weave the flowers together.

I'll make you a crown!

Leaf Collage

Let's find a spot for you.

Leaf Jewelry

Thread leaves and berries on a strong piece of thread to make this lovely necklace.

You can also make a leaf hat.

What a well-dressed bear!

Leaf Puppets

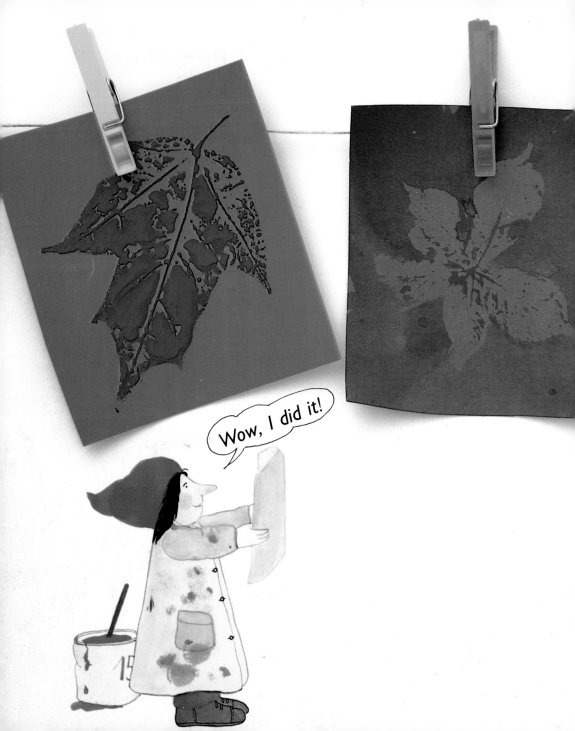

Leaf Printing

Cover a fresh leaf with paint and then press onto a sheet of paper. You can make all kinds of colorful prints.

15. 9. 88

You must use freshly picked leaves, which are rolled up and left to dry. You can use chestnuts or other seeds for their heads.

Would you like to join your family?

A Leaf Family

Tea Time

Knallerbsen

If your leafy friends are thirsty, make them some pretend tea by floating leaves in water.
Or, ask an adult to help you make some real tea. Real tea is made from leaves, too.

Tea time!

Mmm. Looks delicious!

A greedy caterpillar.

May we
join you for tea?

A thirsty crocodile.